SHARK CHUMS

CAN BLUE HIDE?

by Adam Lehrhaupt

illustrated by Pauline Gregory

Ready-to-Read

Simon Spotlight

New York   London   Toronto   Sydney   New Delhi

For Med, I miss our underwater adventures. —A. L.

SIMON SPOTLIGHT

An imprint of Simon & Schuster Children's Publishing Division

1230 Avenue of the Americas, New York, New York 10020

This Simon Spotlight edition August 2022

Text copyright © 2022 by Adam Lehrhaupt

Illustrations copyright © 2022 by Pauline Gregory

For information about special discounts for bulk purchases, please contact Simon &
Schuster Special Sales at 1-866-506-1949 or business@simonandschuster.com.

Manufactured in the United States of America 0722 LAK

10 9 8 7 6 5 4 3 2 1

Cataloging-in-Publication Data for this title is available from the Library of Congress.

ISBN 978-1-6659-0800-9 (hc)

ISBN 978-1-6659-0799-6 (pbk)

ISBN 978-1-6659-0801-6 (ebook)

Shark
can seek.

Seek, Shark, seek.

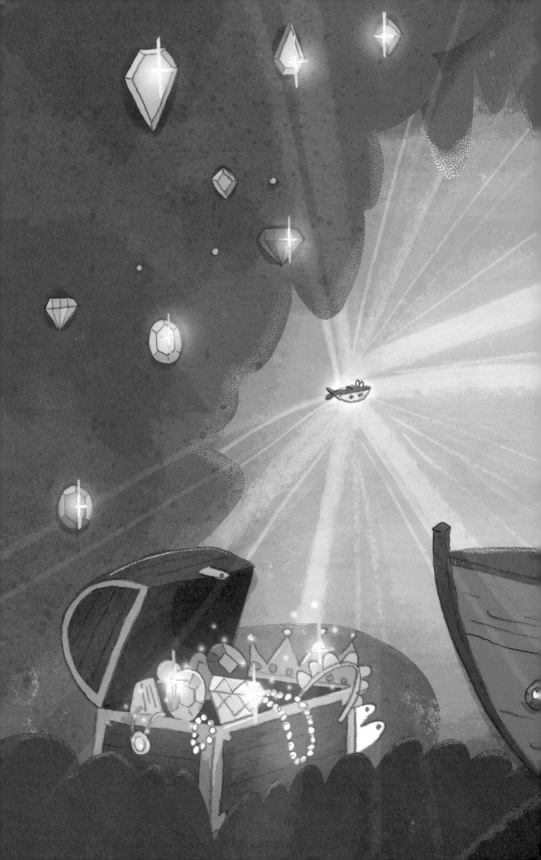

Can Blue hide?

Hide, Blue, hide.

Shark will peek.

Peek.

Peek.

Peek.

Blue hides well . . .

. . . on this shell.

Shark looks near.

Shark looks far.

Nope. Just Star.

Then Shark stares.

Now Shark glares.

Go, Shark, go!

No, Blue, no!

Shark says, "Ewww. . . .

Got you, Blue!"

Now Blue seeks.

And . . . Shark sneaks.